The Other Side of Carroll

by Sophia Nesamoney

Society of Young Inklings

SOCIETY OF YOUNG INKLINGS

The Other Side of Carroll
Copyright © 2013 Sophia Nesamoney

This title is also available as a Society of Young Inklings ebook.
Visit www.younginklings.com/ebooks

Requests for information should be addressed to:
Society of Young Inklings. PO Box 3134, Los Altos, CA 94024

Editor: Naomi Kinsman Downing
Cover Design: Debbie Bakker
Interior Design and Composition: Sarah Lyn Rogers

Printed in the USA
First Printing: September 2013
ISBN 978-0-9839568-9-1

This book is dedicated to my mom, dad, brother, and Patty. And to Sunny, my German Shepherd, who inspired the character of Bronx.

Table of Contents

Prologue

In Bronx, New York, at the corner of Daisy Street in a warm brick house lived a happy family, the Tarks. The mother, Barbara-Ann Tark, spent her days sewing and gardening. She made the best apple pie. The father, Joseph Tark, had traveled all around the world and always had many exciting stories to tell his children. The set of twins named Oliver Joseph Tark and Shirley-Ann Tark always found ways to make trouble, but not too much trouble. Not anything that apple pie and stories by the fire couldn't fix. One summer, the twins were about eight years old, and the family had come back from seeing the movie, *Feathers and Roses*, a family favorite. Their father sent Oliver out to get some bread. Shirley was playing outside with her jump rope, and the parents were talking about something they never talked about in front of the children for dangerous reasons. Just then, something changed the course of all of their lives. Something big, something that could never be fixed.

Chapter One

Oliver

I tried shifting my bags to the other hand, but it was no use. A scraggly fourteen-year-old boy like me couldn't carry even the few bags that I had from The Villa, the orphanage that I had just run away from. I had just escaped Russell Redlock's famous headlock. Even though I knew I could never survive out here, I was willing to take the risk if it meant I would never have to suffer through another headlock again. Besides, right now, Ms. Bellwether, the grumpy old lady who ran the orphanage, would be yelling, "Get in bed, you dirty rags, I'm trying to go to sleep!!"

Chapter One

The outside air was much fresher than the old, hot, stinky orphanage. Even the ground felt better than the beds at the orphanage. I was convinced they were made out of rocks. Also, Ms. Bellwether never bothered to change the gross sheets. All of this thinking about sleeping made me tired, so I set my things down on the cobbled street corner and fell fast asleep.

In the middle of the night, I woke up with a start. I had heard something. I searched the pitch black darkness. What looked like pigeons were now settling on the low branches of a tree, but there was something else, something that made me feel uneasy.

I realized something soft but rugged lay on my right arm. Something gooey was dripping down my left arm. At first I thought a giant pigeon had landed on me and relieved itself—and boy, I hated pigeons—so I screamed, thinking it would fly away. No such luck. It didn't budge. I gathered up all my courage and decided to touch it. The soft, rugged thing was sleeping, right? What harm could it do? What I felt was not what I expected; it was an animal of some sort. Instead of touching feathers, my fingers ran over tangled, smelly fur. On my other arm, I realized that it was drool, not pigeon poo.

But what kind of animal was it?

I worked my way up what felt like its neck, thinking to myself, *How odd, an animal with wet spikes on its neck?*

Then the spikes closed down on my hand. What I thought of as the neck had really been the mouth and before I pulled my hand away, its teeth went through the back of my hand. I looked down at my skin. It was only a tiny cut, but still I started to cry.

Then, the dog licked my face as if to say, *I'm sorry, please don't be mad at me.*

I was about to hit the mutt, and tell him to get lost, but something inside me wouldn't let me do it. Something about his eyes told me he would serve great importance someday. I curled up against him and we both fell asleep, feeling the soothing cool breeze against our cheeks.

When I woke, the busy streets of New York seemed even more crammed and loud than The Villa ever was. People were running around faster than I could count! I must have heard about a billion "Excuse me"s and "Sorry, didn't mean to bump into you"s from people passing by. I kept getting dirty looks from mothers as they passed by and whispered to their obedient children, saying, "Try not to stare, honey, this is what happens when you are lazy and do not obey your parents."

When I tried to stand up, I didn't remember about my cut hand until I crashed into the pigeon-turd covered tree. Pain shot through my arm like a fiery bullet. Okay, I was exaggerating, but it hurt so badly. The mutt had woken up, and I could see he was really dirty. So was I. We both needed a shower. I put my old dog's collar on him so that if I lost him, I would be able to find him again.

We wandered across town, stopping at the bread line to get some bread and milk. Suddenly, I saw a mailman and his wife walking towards their house. I decided to follow them because they might have a shower. I peeked in through their grey curtains, and saw a toilet with yellow liquid all over the seat. Even the shower was rusty.

The mutt howled as if to say, "That will never work."

Down the street, I saw a mom, a couple of girls, and a dad who just happened to be a policeman. I figured that if I could run away from the orphanage, I would be able to run away from him. It sounded crazy even to me, but the mutt and I were desperate. I followed the family to their house, making sure to be very quiet. I had to climb up their brick wall in order to see their bathroom. It looked good, clean, and the mutt nodded his head in approval.

We snuck in behind the second youngest daughter who left the door open just a little crack. We made our way upstairs, found the bathroom, and went inside. Someone had recently been here and had left behind the choking smell of perfume. Making sure that no one else was on the top floor with us, I shut the door. Then, we climbed into the shower. Sludge dripped off the mutt. I scrubbed him and then scrubbed myself. Then, I left him in the shower while I cleaned up the mess we had left on the floor. The tiles looked clean, but now they were too shiny and spotless. With a family that big, their bathroom would never be this clean! It needed to be messier.

Right on cue, the mutt ran out of the shower, with soap and bubbles flying everywhere! The mutt lunged against the door and I realized I had forgotten to lock it as it swung open. He charged down the stairs. I yanked my pants on and ran after him. The stairs were wooden and not carpeted, so it was pretty hard not to slip down them as I tried to catch up to the mutt.

"No! Someone's going to see you!" I hissed.

The mutt kept running as if to say, "Oh, really?"

Then I heard footsteps. I cringed. It was the dad, A.K.A the policeman.

"What do you think you are doing in my house, boy?" he asked me.

His nose was scrunched up and he had lots of forehead wrinkles.

"Leave the poor boy alone, Richard," the mother said.

She smelled like peaches and brown sugar and had on a brown apron that was practically white from something that looked like mashed potatoes. In her arms, she was holding the most adorable baby I had ever seen!

"Now, what are you doing here?" she questioned, her thin, sweet face full of smiles.

"My name is Oliver. I lost my parents. I can't find them," I lied.

"Oh, that's horrible! How about we keep you for the night?" she asked.

For the moment, nothing sounded better, but I later regretted my decision. The mother introduced me to the rest of the family. They had six girls and no boys. Their two-year old daughter, Ellie, was crying in her mother's arms. She had the biggest, roundest, bluest eyes I had ever seen. Susie was five and quite plump, with thick blond curls and a runny nose. She was wearing a pink dress with her name embroidered on it.

At the moment, she was whining at her mother, "I want my food now!"

Their eight-year old, Dorothy, was very skinny and wore a torn green dress and stockings that looked like hand-me-downs.

She had messy braids and said to her mom, "Why can't I go back outside? I don't care about him!"

Like Dorothy, eleven-year old Annie was also quite skinny. They both had brown hair and freckles like their dad, but she was much calmer and more civilized. Unlike Dorothy, she had two neat braids, a blue dress, and she didn't say a word.

The family had a fourteen-year old, named Ruby. She wore a black and white checkered dress, and her cheeks flushed a shade of rose when I smiled at her.

After I smiled at her and her mom told her to stop

staring at me, Ruby said, "Oh my gosh, you guys are so annoying!"

Then she stormed upstairs. The oldest daughter, Elizabeth, was sixteen, and she wore her long, straight blond hair in a big red bow at the back of her head. She was very tall and wore a red dress. She talked and acted like an adult.

The mother gave me the fourteen-year-old girl's room for the night. Big mistake. The room was covered in pink and smelled like the choking perfume that had filled the bathroom. Posters of Frank Sinatra plastered her walls. The worst part was the mutt was going to sleep with the five-year-old brat because she wouldn't let go of baby Ellie's hair until her mother said that she could sleep with *my* dog.

I followed everyone downstairs and they all sat down to eat dinner at the dining room table, everyone except for the fourteen-year-old, who was apparently too mad about having to share her room. Pictures of the family hung on the dining room's light brown walls. It made me sad. I wished I could go back to that time when my family had our pictures on our walls.

"Oliver, honey, you cannot come down here wearing those dirty clothes," the mother said sweetly. "Come upstairs with me. Maybe we can find you something else to wear, okay?"

"Sure," I said.

We walked upstairs and she led me into her room. Rose wallpaper covered the walls and her comforter looked like it was made of velvet.

"Richie doesn't like it when other people wear his clothes, so we will have to work something out," she said.

When she said work it out, I didn't think she meant I would have to dress in her clothes! She gave me a pink button up shirt, a skirt and some white lace socks and underwear. I carried the clothes to the bathroom, my feet dragging the whole way. I put on the shirt, but kept my pants, socks, and underwear on. There was no way I'd wear any more of her stuff. I hobbled downstairs. Something felt uncomfortable, almost as if I had put my clothes on wrong.

"Oliver, come down and eat. Your food is getting cold!" the mother said.

"Coming," I said.

I ran over to the table. In the process, one leg got tangled up with the other and I face-planted into the mashed potatoes, only to look up and see it was the father's plate. He was covered in mashed potato. He even had a mushy white moustache! Though I thought it was amusing, no one else did.

"Eeeeeww, gross! Daddy, don't eat your mashed potatoes now!" Elizabeth said.

"Look, Mommy, he's wearing your shirt inside out," Annie said quietly.

"Hahahahahahaha!" Dorothy said.

I got more laughs.

"He looks just like a penguin!!!" Susie exclaimed.

Then everybody was laughing at me!

Just when I thought matters couldn't get worse, the mutt came bounding down the stairs. I tried to pull my feet in, but it was too late. He came at me full speed, tripped over my foot, and landed on the table, spraying bubbles from the shower everywhere. The dad gave the mom a stern look.

"Hey, Oliver, I think it would be best if you just take your dog and go," the dad said, gritting his teeth.

I ran upstairs and changed back into my clothes. The mutt gave Susie a kiss and we left the house. The night was very dark outside. I was happy to get out of the house, but sad at the same time. How would I ever survive on my own?

We went out to the sidewalk, but then a pack of stray dogs came running down the street straight at us. They were dirty, scarred, and had matted fur. Their big, sharp fangs glistened in the moonlight. I moved out of the way and hid behind a garbage can, but the mutt didn't. They stared at the mutt for about five seconds. I held my breath. As much as I loved the mutt, there was no way I was going out there to save him. The pack sprang at him, scratching his neck with their sharp claws. I squeezed my eyes shut. When I opened them, I saw him running away, whimpering. I wanted to follow him, but it was too dangerous with those stray dogs around. Hopefully, he would be okay.

Chapter Two

Shirley

There aren't many things I am scared of, but that's not what other people think. Street kids tease me singing:

"Shirley, Shirley,

Is a girly,

And her hair is curly, too!"

First of all, I am not girly. Second of all, I would beat them up in seconds, but then they would go cry to their mommies and I would get in trouble. I guess I could just run away, but I keep all of my bags on a cobbled street corner right next to a candy shop--the one I used to go to with my brother, Oliver, before my parents died. Once, every couple of days, I go in and buy a peppermint cone, the way I used to do.

I headed over to the bakery where I worked, kneading dough, making croissants and other pastries. The work was lovely because of the glorious food we got to take home at night, but the pay was terrible. Still, I managed to make a couple of bucks per day. With the money, I allowed myself to buy only one more set of clothes or shoes, or maybe another bag every three months. With the money, I guess I could've eventually moved off the streets, but the house I lived in before had already been sold three years ago. Plus, people would be suspicious if a fourteen-year-old girl moved in without any parents.

I liked the coziness of the street corner where I lived, even though the ground was rough. I had always liked to sleep in corners. I felt as if I had a person on either side of me because of the walls, so I wasn't as lonely. People always try to avoid each other on the streets because they fear that people mean them harm. I couldn't care less because the only things around me were just a couple of stray dogs and the candy shop. Nobody ever bothered me.

The white moon glistened and the stars were starting to come out, so I decided to go to sleep. I curled up with my head in the corner on top of my wool blanket. I carefully lifted the blood soaked photo of my family and then kissed it. That terrible night, I'd already escaped, but then I snuck back inside to find something I'd forgotten and found the picture lying on my bed. I had only been eight, and I was too afraid to wait for my brother. He might have been dead, anyway, and I was sure the murderer would come back for me.

The picture was of my father, Ollie, my mom, and me. We were all smiling in the candy store. Ollie had a handful of toffees. I had a peppermint ice cream cone, and Mother and Father were sharing a candy bar. This was the happiest moment of our lives. Oliver and I were six, so it was two years before my mother and father were killed.

I looked up into the night sky and at the pigeon turd covered tree. I was lonely and wished I could have someone to understand me. Someone my age, maybe even a friend?

The next day, since I didn't have to work, I decided to go to the candy shop. I strolled in. The candy shop had creamy white walls that looked like meringues, red and white checkered tables, and a counter with all of the candy

I could ever want. It always smelled like fudge and banana cream pies! What I found was surprising. Mr. Carroll was fast asleep, but someone else was behind the counter.

"May I have a peppermint cone, please?" I asked in my sweetest voice.

"Um, ur uh well, bye," the boy said, as he shot out of the candy shop with a handful of toffees.

"Mr. Carroll, Mr. Carroll, wake up! Some boy has stolen toffees!"

Mr. Carroll awoke with a start, and screamed right in my face, "What happened?!"

"A boy was stealing! He stole a handful of toffees. I think he was about my age, but I couldn't really see his face," I said, twirling my curls, as I always did when I was nervous.

"I think I might've seen him around before. Humph, he causes me way too much trouble," said Mr. Carroll, deep in thought.

"Sorry to interrupt your thoughts, Mr. Carroll, but can I get a peppermint cone, please?" I asked.

"Sure. Well, thanks anyway for telling me, Shirley!" he said.

He handed me the peppermint cone. It was a sugar

cone with pink ice cream and peppermint chunks. Mmm, my favorite! Mr. Carroll was always such a nice man who gave his customers anything they wanted. I wished that people wouldn't steal from him.

My mother had said when I was younger, "Stealing is wrong, Shirley." And she was right.

Chapter Three

Oliver

I walked along to get some bread from the bread lines. The streets weren't too crowded, but I sort of wished the mutt were there with me. When I was younger, my parents had warned me about strangers taking boys and girls.

Since I was away from the mutt, I decided I should try and enjoy myself and be free, something I could never do at the orphanage. When I was little, before my parents died, they would take my sister, Shirley, and me to the movies and then we would go to the candy shop right next door. Shirley had always loved the movies, though I thought they were boring. Shirley disappeared when I was eight. Disappeared, *not* died. At least, I didn't see her dead before they took me away to the orphanage. Someday, I hope to find her, but it will be very hard because she has probably changed in the last six years. I can remember a bright sunny day, when the birds were chirping and the lilies were blooming. I was eight and Mother and Father had sent me to get some bread, but we didn't have to get it from the bread line because we were rich.

I came home that day with a loaf of bread and a peppermint ice cream cone, laughing and singing my favorite tune, when I called for my parents and nobody answered.

"Father, I have your bread!" I yelled, a little louder this time, but again, no answer.

I figured they were probably sleeping or maybe putting Shirley to bed for her afternoon nap, which she still had the habit of doing even though she was eight years old. So I went upstairs to Shirley's room. Nobody, just a cone of peppermint ice cream splattered on the floor.

"Shirley," I shouted, "Mother and Father are going to kill you!!"

Our parents hated it when their floor got messy. Shirley

didn't answer, so I went to Mother and Father's room.

It was strangely quiet. The floor creaked whenever I moved. I opened the door just a crack--they weren't there. I walked in, and the clock's ticking sped up as if it were waiting for me to do something. I was scared. Where were my parents? Then I saw the trail of blood leading to their closet. With my heart thudding, I followed the trail into their closet. It was dark, so I turned on the light. When I looked down at my feet, there were my mother and father, lying on the floor: Mother with a bullet in her side, and Father with two bullets in the center of his chest.

I started to cry, feeling as if something had been sucked out of me, something big. Blood leaked out of them and by now their clothes were covered in blood. But I noticed something else. In mother's hand was a small picture soaked with blood, not because of the bullet, but because of the glass, making a deep wound into her hand.

The picture she was clutching was of my father, her, Shirley, and me. We were all smiling in the candy store and I had a handful of toffees. Shirley had a peppermint ice cream cone, and mother and father were sharing a candy bar.

I carefully removed the glass from her cut and took

the blood soaked picture out of the frame. The bullets had destroyed everything else in the room. But the other thing I noticed about Mother was that she was lying oddly on her side. I felt her hands, which were still warm. Father's were stone cold, There was no hope of them still being alive. I rolled Mother over onto her back. Then the way she was lying made sense. She had been protecting her favorite necklace, the one I had given her last year on her birthday. A bitter tear rolled down my face, followed by another, and then many more tears. Why did this have to happen to them? Who was going to take care of me? Where was my sister?

I noticed something else: a red bandana on the floor. Instead of having checkers or something on it, it had an eagle. Maybe the murderer could have worn this bandana, but it fel off when he was running away. I took the necklace, gave them each a kiss on the cheek, and said a final goodbye to my parents. Then I noticed that Charlotte, our dog, was standing right next to me. I grabbed her by the collar, thinking she might lead me to Shirley or help me, but instead she pulled out of the collar and ran away.

I was left with only her collar.

I thought about chasing after her, but I was panicked,

thinking, *What if Shirley is dead, too?*

When I got to her room, I couldn't make myself look at her closet. I did not want to see another dead body in there if there was one. I finally gathered up my courage and searched her room, but there was no sign of Shirley and no blood. The only sign of her was a huge crack in her window, big enough that she could have fit through. I lay the photo on her bed. Maybe she would come back for it and realize I'd been here too. Then I ran out of my creepy house

I ran into the candy shop. Since I had been very little, the candy shop had been my place of comfort. The shop always smelled so good, like my childhood. My family and I used to come to the candy shop very often, but for some odd reason my mother never let me talk to the owner, who was usually at the cash register.

That day, I scooped up a handful of toffees and hid in the corner waiting for someone I knew to pass by and take pity on me, but nobody ever did. After a few hours, I gathered up my courage and decided to go back home. I glanced through the window. Everything seemed the same as it had been before, creepy and quiet.

I went up to Shirley's room. The photo was gone, but

there was a note that said:

Dear Ollie,

I hope you don't mind, I took the photo. I do not know when we

will meet again as I have left. I love you.

Love, Shirley

I wondered why she would write me a letter instead of coming to get me. I felt betrayed. Didn't she care about me?

The next day I came back to see if Shirley had returned, but no Shirley. The only thing I noticed was the bandana was gone. A few days later, the police found me when I was asleep in the candy shop, and they delivered me to the orphanage.

"Hey! Watch it, jerk," someone said.

In surprise, I crashed into him and quickly snapped out of my memory. I looked up at the man. He was fat and he wore ugly pants with holes in them. He had a dirty, unshaven face and a glimmering golden tooth. He also had a red bandana.

"That's strange," I thought. That was the red bandana I had seen when my parents were shot. Could he have had something to do with it?

Just then, the mutt trotted up behind me, but once he saw the man's face, he started to run in the opposite direction.

The man's expression changed from a frown to a threatening scowl.

"I will come back for you!"

The mutt started to bark viciously at the man.

"Yes, you!" said the man

Could he have meant me? There was something familiar about this man. He made me uncomfortable, so I ran as fast as I could in the direction of the candy store. After I slipped inside, I got some toffees, waited until I was sure he was gone, and then I went back to my street corner.

Chapter Four

Shirley

On my last free day of the week, I decided to go to the Gladys R Randall library. It was a cold, gloomy day and leaves flew at my face. The warmth of the library greeted me as I burst through the door. As soon as I stepped inside, the three grumpy librarians, Wanda, Patsy, and Gladys, started whispering about me.

"Tell Gladys that I told you to tell her to tell that girl to stop running in the library," said Wanda to Patsy.

Wanda was pretty tall, had short brown hair, and was wearing a way too small brown dress. She wore black boots.

"Wanda told me to tell you to tell the girl to stop running in the library," Patsy said to Gladys.

Patsy was the tallest out of the three of them, about five feet, seven inches. She had long blond hair with streaks of grey, tied up in a braided bun. She was wearing a light pink dress that was way too big for her. She also wore light pink ballet flats.

" S S S S S T T T T T O O O P P P P RRRRUUUUNNNNNIIIINNNNNGGG   IN   MY LIIIBBBRAAAARRY!!!!!" said Gladys, the leader of their trio and the owner of the library, which was named after her.

She was very short, only about four feet tall! She stood on a chair and stared at me as I stopped running. She had mid-length thin hair that was tied up in a high, side ponytail. She wore too much pink blush and had glasses that looked like they were going to slip off her nose any second now. She wore a canary yellow shirt with blue polka dots on it, a tight navy blue skirt, and bright pink high heels that made her look about half a foot taller.

"Sorry," I said.

"Tell Gladys that I told you to tell her to tell the girl to stop talking in the library," Wanda whispered to Patsy.

"Wanda told me to tell you to tell the girl to stop talking in the library," said Patsy to Gladys.

" S S S S S T T T T T O O O O P P P P P P TTTTAAAAALLLLKKKKING IIIIINNNN MMMMMYYYYY LLLLIBBBBBRRRRAAARRRYYYY!!!!!!!!!!" Gladys screamed.

"Sorry!" I whispered as I made my way to the back of the library where the encyclopedias were.

I looked over at the books. They still hadn't bought new ones. All they had were *The Encyclopedia of T-R* and *The Encyclopedia of A-D*. I had read both books, so I closed my eyes and picked randomly. It must have been a really slimy book because it weirdly felt like a dog tongue. I opened my eyes and was surprised to see the cutest puppy ever. He had a wiry greyish black coat, and his paws were way too big for him. He stuck his tongue out at me, tilted his head and gave me a puppy smile. It was love at first sight. Then I reached my arm out at him and he took it as a treat. His mouth lunged at my arm and clamped down.

"Owwwwwwww!!!" I screamed.

"WHAT IN THE NAME OF BOOKS IS GOING ON THERE?!!" Gladys screamed.

The three librarians speed-walked down to where I was.

"IT'S A DOG!!!" Patsy tried to scream, but her soft voice faded away.

"I'll get him," Wanda said.

She leaped for the bookshelf but the puppy was already out. She hit her hard head on the bookshelf.

"Is this your dog, Suley?" questioned Gladys.

"It's Shirley," I corrected her, "and yes, he is my dog."

"Yes, that's what I said, Suley!!!" she said, as if I was crazy to correct her.

"Let's think of a plan!" Wanda said.

They formed a huddle and started "whispering" even though I could still hear them from about ten feet away.

"We should take his ears..." Patsy sang.

Gladys and Wanda had serious expressions on their faces. I could see that Wanda's forehead was starting to get a little bump from when she crashed into the bookshelf. Now that I took a better look at Gladys, she didn't look very old at all. She looked ancient, like king Tut. She had to be ancient because the library was even named after her.

".....and we will tie them in a knot and tie them in a

bow!" Patsy sang, sounding like a dying horse.

"No, we should make him read books for the rest of his life!" exclaimed Wanda.

I couldn't help laughing at that one. Seeing that they were occupied, I scooped the puppy up. His warm furry head rested on my shoulder and his warm wet nose sniffed my neck. I made my way to the back exit, hoping that they wouldn't notice that I was walking away.

Right when I got to the door, I heard Gladys screaming again.

"WHAT IN THE NAME OF BOOKS DO YOU THINK YOU ARE DOING? YOU FOOLS, THE GIRL AND THE DOG ARE GETTING AWAY!!!!"

I ran out the door as fast as I could and didn't stop running until I reached my street corner.

It was then that I saw that the puppy had a long, deep wound in his neck. I took off his collar and tore off some of my dress and patched up the wound using the sewing kit that my mother and father gave me for my eighth birthday.

Chapter Five

Oliver

After I ate about half of the toffees, I fell asleep and didn't wake up until the morning. I was sort of sad that the dog was gone, but I had no idea how to find him now.

I headed over to the bread line and got some food. I loved the bread lines, seeing the warm doughy bread being cut out and put on plates. Once I got my slice, I savored it, feeling the warm bread touch my desperate mouth. I forgot all of my worries, all of my fears, and the fact that I was freezing. Then, I went to the candy shop, and exchanged the coins that I had saved up from my birthday money at the orphanage for five dollars, which he handed me, I thanked him, making sure to not show the owner my face because he might recognize me as the person who stole the toffees. Then I went to the movie theater.

I asked the man in the ticket booth how much it would be to watch the movie. He told me, and I was in luck! I could afford it. I gave him the money and walked in. I found a nice seat up in the middle row in the center. I couldn't really tell what the movie theater looked like, or who was sitting next to me, because it was too dark. The movie was about a man and his big, happy, rich family. They reminded me of our family except nobody disappeared or died at the end. Tears trickled down my face. Finally I couldn't take it anymore and I had to leave. On my way out of the theatre, I bumped into a man with a large moustache and a red bandana with an eagle on his neck. He looked like the same man I had seen before.

After that, I was so depressed because of the happy family part of the movie. I wished that my family were still like that. I sulked around to the bread line to get more bread. Then I walked back to the corner to look for the dog, but there was no dog. Just my bags and the tree. So I went back to the candy shop and one of the signs in the window announced a fair just a couple streets down.

I walked to the fair. For kids it was free, and I was pretty short, so I passed right by the paying booth. I looked around. The fair was full of little kids running around and playing games.

"A game ought to cheer me up," I thought.

So I tossed the coins into the hoops and I actually made it into all three. The man gave me a notebook as a prize. Then I hurried along to the horses. I had always loved to ride on horses since I was little. There were two horses that must have been carried there by a truck because I didn't see a stable anywhere.

I mounted a horse named Midnight with the help from a big guy with a moustache hoisting me up. The horse's coat was a midnight black and his mane was a fluffy white, just like the marshmallow crème I always see at the candy store, piled high on the lemon cakes in pretty designs. I held onto the horse as the man walked behind us. The horse was at a gentle walk, but even then it was so exciting. For once since my parents had died, I actually smiled and laughed like a little child.

I dismounted and walked over to the cotton candy, where I saw the light and airy spun sugar ready for someone to buy it. The only problem was that nobody stood behind the cash register. Just then, I had an idea.

"I could hide behind the display, then put my money into the cash register, and take one then. It would work, and I wouldn't even have to steal!!" I whispered to myself.

I hid behind the display until everyone was out of sight. Then I made my way to the register and clicked the "open" button. To my anger, the drawer made a ringing sound. I heard footsteps coming. I bolted across the room, opened the front door, and hid in the empty saltwater taffy barrel, covering myself with my jacket. I closed the lid on the top just in time.

"Oh darn, that brain of mine, it's getting way too old to even function. I mean, am I really crazy? Didn't the cash registe- oh, there I am, talking to myself again," I heard an old lady say with a slight southern accent.

"Oh well, I guess I'd better close it for the night. Don't want any rats coming in here eating my goods," the old lady said, talking to herself once again.

Then, I heard a door slam, a key turn, and I knew I

was locked in the cotton candy shack on the fair grounds for the night.

Chapter Six

Shirley

The puppy and I woke up at eight a.m. I could tell the time from the clock on the candy shop wall, which was right next to my street corner. I was really late for work. Panicked, I ran my fingers through my hair since I didn't have time to look for my comb. I hurried over to the bakery and went inside with the puppy since I didn't have time to put him anywhere else. How much trouble could he really be?

The bakery always smelled like sugar and dough, partly because Jerry always managed to get some on the walls, which I had to clean up! The shop had white and black checkered walls and black chairs.

When I got there, Jerry sighed. "Man, Shirley, how late can you be?"

When I didn't respond, he said, "What's the matter, cat got your tongue?"

"Don't mind him, Shirley. Jerry just doesn't know how to be nice!" said Ruth, looking at the mutt in an odd way.

"It's ok, Ruthie," I said.

Even though her name was Ruth, I always called her Ruthie. Ever since I started working here, it had been a big hassle with Ruth and Jerry. They're cousins, so they were always yelling at each other as if they were brother and sister.

I tied the puppy to the metal pole inside right by the entrance and told him to stay. Then I went down the hall and through the door to the bathroom. When I came back, Jerry and Ruth were rolling out the dough for bread and the mutt was gone.

"Where did he go?" I asked in a panicked voice that came out more like a squeak. I looked out the window. No puppy. I looked under the tables. No puppy. I looked everywhere. NO PUPPY!

"Ur um he um..." Ruth started.

Jerry cut her off. "He ran away."

Both of their faces turned bright red, like a tomato. I couldn't believe it. My face was flaming,

"You just let him run away?! You think he's some kind of joke! Well, to me he's no-"

"Calm down, Shirley," Ruth said.

There was no calming down now. He was my little baby! He could be hurt! Instead of yelling back at them again, I decided that I should stop yelling so I kept my head down and started kneading dough.

During lunch, Ruthie and Jerry went off for a little bit together by themselves and then they came back and then sat down next to me. Ruthie sat on my right side, and Jerry on my left.

We ate our lunches silently. I was still thinking about my poor little puppy, lost somewhere without someone to love him.

Chapter Seven

Oliver

When I woke up, I realized I had fallen asleep in the barrel. I rubbed my sore shoulders and looked around. The store looked like a mini shop and was made of wood. Once I finally got out of the saltwater taffy barrel, I ran out the entrance. The lady from yesterday had just come in and was now making the cotton candy by the entrance. Now that I got a good look at her, I noticed that she wasn't just old. She must have been ancient. Even her bare feet had wrinkles. She stood about four and a half feet tall and was very plump. I shuffled to the entrance and snuck back to the customer side of the counter without her noticing.

Now, I looked like any other shopper. Well, one who looked like they were half starved and had a bad hair day. Boy, I could sure use some cotton candy. The thing was, I had already put all my money in the register the day before.

Then I had an idea.

"Waaaaaah, WAAAH," I started to fake cry. The lady looked up from the sugar and immediately her face melted.

"Oh, my dear sweet love, what's the matter?" she asked.

"I don't know where my mommy is!" I exclaimed, making my eyes water.

"Oh, my poor pumpkin. Well, I know just the thing to make you feel better," she said.

I was so excited, I was about to jump out of my skin. My plan was working!

She came back with a pencil and said, "Honey, I just knew it would make you happy. Everyone just loves school!"

I looked at her like she was crazy for a little too long.

"Oh, I'm sorry, darling. You don't like it? What would make you happy?" she questioned.

"Well, I'm kinda hungr-" she didn't let me finish.

"Well, my sweetcakes, I just made some cotton candy, would you care to try some?"

"Yes, please," I sniffled.

The lady handed me five sticks of blue cotton candy, and I wolfed them down before she could ask me another question. Then, out of the corner of my eye I saw a mutt running just outside the fairgrounds past the last tent. Could it be my mutt? I thanked the lady, claimed to have seen my mother, and ran off.

As soon as I got closer, I could see it *was* my mutt. He ran towards me and I felt real tears coming. Then he rubbed his head against my leg. Someone had fixed his neck because it was all patched up. We sat on the side of the road and I rubbed his ears while he drooled on the sidewalk making a puddle right underneath him. I didn't mind the drool, I was just glad he was back.

We got in the bread line and got some bread, but then something scary happened.

A man with a large overcoat and a red bandana, the one that kept stalking me, bumped into me and said, "I'll come back for you later," in a deep voice that made my insides shiver.

Chapter Eight

Shirley

I woke up too early this morning because the bakery had the most complicated order ever. I was so worried, I couldn't go back to sleep! One customer had ordered ten cakes, each a different flavor (strawberry, cinnamon, vanilla, chocolate, lemon, marble, carrot, mango mousse, orange spice, and red velvet), twenty cupcakes, each with a separate design, and three loaves of cinnamon bread by noon, all for their banquet, which you had to pay to attend!

As I walked to the bakery, I kept my arms tucked into to my chest, for it was almost winter, and I could already see windows covered in a thin layer of frost, and the trees were already bare. The wind was strong, and I could feel it through my coat. I was glad when I finally slipped inside the bakery, but instead of the fresh smell of dough, sugar, and lemon, there was the smell of artificial cleaner. Ruth and Jerry sat at one of the tables, whispering.

"What do you think you are doing?! We've got four hours to get this big order in!" I shouted.

My face was hot and red with anger. If we didn't get this order done in time, or we messed it up, I could be fired by Roberto, the owner!

First they let my dog go, then they acted like our big order was no big deal.

"Am I the only one who does any work around here?"

I was so mad, instead of yelling back at me, they walked up to the kitchen and started to make the dough for the bread. I started on the cakes. After two hours, I was done baking and frosting all of the cakes, and Ruth and Jerry were still on their first loaf of cinnamon bread. I was a mess. I had flour all over me!

Though I was busy, I couldn't help but notice that Ruth and Jerry were still whispering. I wanted to know what they were talking about. I mean, even though I was about eight years younger than them, they could trust me with a secret, couldn't they? I was so into my thoughts that when Ruth called my name, I jumped and didn't respond directly.

"Shirley," Ruth began.

I snapped out of my daydream, because she seemed mad, or irritated, or both.

"Yeah," I said.

"You're... um... uh... spilling all the batter on your shirt," Ruth replied.

"Oh," I said, as I caught the glass bowl just in time before it smashed to the ground.

Then, a sharp edge of the glass cut my hand. I wiped it off on my sleeve, forgetting that the batter was still on it. Now, I had blood-covered batter all over my shirt and hands, not to mention how much my hand hurt.

"Shirley, are you okay?" Ruth asked.

"Sure," I replied, trying not to show any emotion.

With the way Ruth was treating me, she didn't deserve for me to tell her anything. Anyway, she'd probably tell Jerry everything I would have said.

"Shirley, can I talk to you?" Ruth asked.

Without replying, I went down to the sink in the cellar and washed all the blood and batter off. I was about to leave when I heard voices coming from upstairs. They seemed to be saying my name. I pressed my ear against the low ceiling, and I could make out two voices, Ruth and Bruce, the cashier boy, but I couldn't tell what they were saying.

"How do you know?" *whisper, whisper.*

"Do you think we should tell Roberto?"

"No," *whisper,* "It's Shirley's business, if Shirley wants to tell him, she can. I feel so bad for her, I mean, she's been living with it all along," *whisper...*

Wait, why was Ruth talking to Bruce, who was even younger than me? He was twelve! Also, what were they talking about? Could they be talking about me living on a street corner? How did they know? My palms started to sweat like crazy.

Were they going to tell Roberto, the manager? If he found out, he would fire me. He would think that I was a dirty slob and that I didn't work hard enough, and he would never understand if I told him what happened to my parents!

Chapter Nine

Oliver

Today the mutt and I woke up at about six a.m. because of the icy winds. Though the mutt was warm and furry, it was getting to be winter, and the cold was much worse than either he or I could bear. I decided to go find a coat that would last me throughout the cold season.

We walked up to the coat shop, with my hands scrunched into my chest, and the mutt scratching the thin layer of frost of off his fur. Finally, we got there, and I read the sign that said *WELCOME TO EUGENE'S COAT SHOP*, in faded grey letters. I strolled into the shop. I felt gloomy. Everything was grey.

"Can I help you, young man?" a voice asked.

I nearly jumped out of my skin. I hadn't noticed the man before. Tall and skinny, he had a crooked beard and grey eyes. He looked as if he belonged in a graveyard. However, he must have been Eugene, the owner of the shop.

"No, sir. Just looking around," I said, trying to look serious like him.

I walked to the back of the shop. The coats looked old and grey, just like Eugene. I pushed through the crowded racks of dusty coats, sneezing; they were all covered in a thick layer of grey dust. Then, a sign caught my eye, in the way back of the shop. It read *NEW COATS* in grey letters.

I ran over to it, but to my dismay, there were the same grey coats, just a bit more expensive and newer. Then, something else caught my eye. It was a beautiful winter coat with tan leather on the outside. On the inside, it was covered in warm animal fur which was tan as well. The coat seemed to shine in the dull grey shop. The coat would be perfect!

I looked up at the sign above me, which read DONATED COATS. *Why?* I wondered. *Why would somebody donate this jacket?*

I decided it didn't matter why, so I walked over to the counter and asked the man how much it cost. When he told me, I couldn't believe the price. Somebody must have gotten it from a really fancy store and then donated it.

Even though the coat was nice, I didn't think it was worth that much money. Besides, I didn't have that much money anyway. Before I could take the jacket back, the man asked me for my full name. He said somebody who looked like me had donated the coat. I wondered why he would need to know. My name was my own business.

Still, I answered, "Joseph Oliver Tark."

The man gave me a puzzled look and I sighed. I should have made up a name. But instead of asking me questions, or accusing me of being a runaway, he studied the label on the coat.

I didn't understand why, and was even more surprised when he said suddenly, "Oh, well, I'm sorry. You can have this coat for free."

He handed the coat over to me like it was worth nothing.

"Thank you, sir," I said as I walked out of the store with

the mutt. I looked on the coat label to see what had made him give me the coat so suddenly. The label read, "Joseph Tark." I shivered. My dad's coat.

Because I was really hungry, I decided to go to the candy shop. This time when I went in, I ordered a peppermint sundae. I still had a little money saved up because the lady at the orphanage gave us money on our birthdays. I watched the shop owner make it for me. I hadn't thought about it before, but he looked a lot like my grandpa, only much older, and the last time I saw my grandpa, he didn't have a beard.

While I was waiting, the man who'd been showing up everywhere came up from behind me, swatted the mutt on the neck, and glared at us. I couldn't tell if he was glaring at the mutt or me. He must have been a really stupid man because the mutt growled and charged at him. Then the mutt ripped a hole in his jeans. I tried to reach for the mutt's collar, but when I stood up, my legs buckled underneath me.

"Back off, you ugly thing, just because I didn't get it this time, doesn't mean you can stop me forever, Charlotte. That thing could have some treasures!" the creepy man said to the mutt, and then ran off.

Why would he do that? What did he mean by a treasure,

and who was Charlotte? Finally, all the pieces clicked into place for me. This guy's bandana was red with an eagle on it, the same one I had seen when I ran into my parent's room after they had gotten shot. He couldn't be their murderer, could he? I decided that I didn't want to think about that. There was something scary about this guy. I knew he wanted something from me or the mutt. Whatever it was, I was not going to give him one little thing, not if I could help it.

Chapter Ten

Shirley

I finally found the mutt today. He was on the other side of the candy shop next to some dirty canvas bags. I figured he might be trying to break them open, so I took him back to my corner with me, because who knew who owned those canvas bags? People weren't very nice to mutts, especially when people found mutts digging around in their stuff. And I didn't want to have to patch the mutt up again after someone else hurt him. Plus, I'd been looking for him everywhere, and I wanted him back.

Maybe I couldn't take him to work with me, because I

couldn't trust Ruth and Jerry not to chase him off, but after work I could take better care of the mutt than he could take care of himself. And it was nice to have a warm, furry pillow at night when it was so cold. I gave him some bread to show him how happy I was that he was back.

About an hour later, I was really hungry, so I decided to go to the candy shop. It was a nice day, so I decided to take the long way around the back with the mutt. We were walking past a few trashcans when a man wearing a police uniform with a red bandana and nametag that said VICTOR VEER came up to me.

"Hello, honey," he said to me, in a scary, deep voice, revealing a golden tooth.

What did he want from me?

"Hi," I replied.

The mutt's ears went back, and he started to growl.

"Back off!" The policeman said.

"I'm so sorry, my dog is just a little restless today," I said to the policeman. Then to the mutt I whispered, "Stop it, sit!"

"Where's the dog's tag?" he asked me.

"Oh, um it's at home, I uh forgot to put it on him," I

said, hoping he would believe me.

"Oh, really? Well then, the next time I see you, you'd better have the dog and his tags," he said, glaring at me.

"I really must get going. My mother is waiting for me," I said.

"How old are you?" he asked me.

"Um, my birthday is tomorrow but right now I am sixteen," I lied, twirling my curls.

My mother once told me that it was better to be older and more respected than younger and childish. The truth was, I was only fourteen but my birthday actually was tomorrow.

"Your mom must not feed you well," he snorted back.

"Oh yes, I am terribly small for my age," I replied.

"Next time I see you, you'd better bring your mom and birth certificate. Oh, and your dog and his tags!" he said to me.

"Sure, I mean... Yes, sir. I will have the dog tags next time," I said, running away.

I finally made my way to the candy shop, where I ordered a peppermint cone with strawberries and whipped cream. I sat down at the counter on a tall stool. I chatted a bit with Mr. Carroll, and then left the shop and walked back to my street corner with the mutt. I had to think of how to get the mutt some tags, and more importantly, how to avoid this creepy Victor guy. There was something familiar about him, but I couldn't put a finger on it. I cuddled up next to the mutt and tried to think about solutions to all of my problems, but instead, I just fell fast asleep.

Chapter Eleven

Oliver

I woke up at about five a.m. this morning because, I couldn't believe it, it was my birthday! The best day ever! It was then that I looked over to my right side and saw that the mutt wasn't there. This frustrated me because I had just found the mutt. Oh well, he probably just went to go find some food. He would be back soon. But, I promised myself I wasn't going to let it ruin my day.

I headed over to the bread line, got some bread and milk, and then I realized I had forgotten my coat. I ran back to my corner but when I was only a few feet away, I saw that scary guy standing right by the candy shop, on the side of the street that I lived on. I stopped dead in my tracks.

He had a police uniform with a nametag that read VICTOR VEER. He was looking down at his shoes and smoking a cigarette. He didn't seem to have noticed me, so I snuck away as quietly as possible. Then, I accidentally banged into a signpost. I saw him drop his cigarette and look up, but I sprinted around the corner before he could really see me. I peeked around the corner, watching, but he didn't seem to know which way I had gone. Eventually, he left, and I went back to get my coat.

Since it was my birthday today, I decided to go to the candy shop, and treat myself to something yummy. I walked in and ordered one blueberry mousse with vanilla ice cream on the side. I also ordered a blueberry smoothie. I sat down at a table with red and white checkers on it. When my food came, I waited for a minute, admiring my plate. It looked like a fairy tale, with the ice cream staying perfect and not melting, the mousse looking so dainty and delicate as if it were a fairy, and the smoothie with just a tiny dollop of whipped cream and a chocolate biscuit dipped in the cream, looking like fairy wings. It was delicious! After I was finished, I wiped my mouth with a napkin, and left feeling like a fairy tale myself.

That night, I reflected on my life. I had the best life when I was little, going to movies and sharing peppermint ice cream with Shirley. Then my parents died when I was eight, and I never saw Shirley again. Now I was fifteen, the age where I could be free. I could be strong. I could be independent. Of course I wasn't an adult yet, but I was no longer a little kid any more. Instead of feeling happy or even brave, though, I felt like a lost mutt, with no guidance and nothing to live for.

I missed my family, but the person I missed the most was Shirley. Then it struck me. Shirley would also be turning fifteen today... Well, if she were still alive. I didn't think she was, though, because by now, wouldn't she have come looking for me? It had been seven years!

Chapter Twelve

Shirley

I slept in today, for it was my birthday. Today, I was fifteen! Because it was my birthday, I had a half-day off of work. So, I ate a loaf of bread from my bag and then I walked down over to the movie theater with the mutt.

"Well, well, well, if it isn't Miss Queen Seventeen," said a deep voice.

I didn't even have to look up to know who it was: Victor Veer.

"Oh, do I know you?" I questioned, keeping my head down.

"Oh yes, I believe we have met, and you can't make me think you are seventeen," he snarled.

"My mom is terribly concerned, but it seems I just don't get enough to eat," I said, raising my head.

"Where's that birth certificate and your parents?" he asked.

"Well, I didn't know I would be seeing you, and my parents are away," I said.

"Well then, what about the dog and his tags?" he questioned.

"Oh, um... he didn't want to put on his collar today. Got to go!" I said, trying to sound strong as I ran past him.

"Don't let me catch you alone again, girl, or I'll put you in an orphanage or something worse!" he screamed at me.

Now I was really scared of the Victor Veer guy, but I had an idea. I was going to have to disguise myself as a boy, so I would look totally different.

Though I knew stealing was wrong, I knew there were times when it was necessary. I snuck into the back of the bread line, where there were clothes that were getting delivered to The Villa. I had heard rumors that the old orphanage had so many kids that it was eight kids per cardboard box. I'm pretty sure the kids didn't sleep in boxes, but I still felt bad stealing clothes from them. I found some old knickerbockers, a shirt and a cap, with some worn out boy's shoes, and ran to the bakery, and put the shirt and knickerbockers on under my work dress, and then I hid the cap and the shoes in the bushes.

After I was finished with my work at the bakery, I slipped off my dress and work shoes, and put them in the bush, then I tied my hair into a bun, tucked it into the cap, put on my shoes, and ran back to my street corner, hoping no one would recognize me.

Chapter Thirteen

Oliver

I was really tired from having fun yesterday on my birthday, so I woke up at about noon. My first thought was, *I'm really hungry.*

I tried to head over to the candy shop, but I tripped over my blanket and fell flat on my face. I was so hungry that I didn't care about the dirt, so I unwrapped my blanket, left it behind, and ran into the candy shop.

The chime rang as the door opened and I looked around for the shopkeeper, but he was not at the counter. Instead, he was reading the newspaper with the radio on really loudly. So, I decided... Why waste my money when this sleepy man isn't paying any attention?

I walked over to the counter and my fingers were centimeters away from the cinnamon rolls. They were elegantly swirled into spirals with fat blobs of icing on top.

I was about to grab one when I heard, "Could you get me a glass of water?" from the old man.

Since this man clearly didn't see me come in, he must have thought I was his helper, Johnny, who looked nothing like me. But, I guess if you're that old, you can be easily fooled.

So, I found a glass in the sink behind the counter and poured him a glass of water. I handed it to him and he asked me for a napkin, so I went all the way back behind the counter an got him five napkins so he couldn't complain anymore.

Then he asked me for some taffy and some peppermint cookies, so I walked behind the counter where the cookies were stored and I picked up two cookies and put them on a plate and then I went over to the jar of taffy. But to my dismay, the taffies were all moldy and gross.

"Um... sir, the taffy is growing mold," I said to him.

"Oh, well then, boy, could you be so kind as to make me another batch?" Mr. Carroll asked.

I'm not quite sure why, but I decided to make a new batch for him. First, I hung up my new coat on the rack. Because he still thought I was Johnny Kirks, maybe he might even pay me!

I started on the taffy. I knew how to make it because when I was younger, my mother and I would always make taffy for Shirley. I had memorized the recipe by heart, so I didn't need to look at the book. I added in to the saucepan about two cups of sugar, one cup of corn syrup, one and a quarter teaspoons salt, two tablespoons butter, one quarter teaspoon peppermint, and seven drops of strawberry juice to make it pink, and then took it off of the heat and let it cool.

Then, I buttered my hands and knotted, pulled, and twisted the taffy, until it was hard to pull, and the pink was starting to fade. I ripped about a quarter off and cut it into tiny pieces, and put it on a pretty pink and yellow floral plate along with some cookies. I took the plate over to the table. When I looked up, he was holding my coat in his hands and drinking a glass of lemonade.

"Oh, why thank you for the treats, Joseph. You may

have some too. Oh, and I made you some lemonade," the man said.

I stared at his face in shock. My palms started to sweat.

"Um, you're welcome. How do you know my name?" I questioned.

"Well, it says it on the jacket. Now is that what you would like to be called? I know it can be confusing with your father having the same name," he said calmly.

I was starting to shake. This was probably some trap to get me back to the orphanage!

"Oliver would be great, Mr. Carroll. But my father and mother are dead. How do you know about my father, anyway?" I questioned.

"Well, let's just say that for you there's no more calling me Mr. Carroll. It'll be Grandpa," he said.

"What?" I asked.

"Ollie, I'm your grandpa," he told me,

I saw a tear of happiness trickle down his check.

Suddenly I couldn't control my emotions. I leapt into his arms and wouldn't let go, crying all of the sadness out of my body while he cried too.

Chapter Fourteen

Shirley

I woke up feeling cheerful! The sun was out, and the birds were chirping, and the mutt and I were having a breakfast of strawberry muffins and fresh fruit, which I had gotten from the bakery yesterday. At about seven thirty, I pinned my hair up, and stuffed the cap over my head. Then, I told the mutt to stay and I skipped over to the bakery.

When I got there, I realized the mutt was still following me, so I said, "Scram, get out of here before somebody sees you!"

The mutt tilted his head and whined. I stared at him until he got the message and left. I felt kind of bad, but it was my job to protect him.

I ran over to the bush and looked for the dress. It was gone! In panic, I peeked inside the bakery. Ruth and Jerry were kneading dough, and right beside Ruth was my work dress, clean and folded. Next to it were my work shoes, polished and shined.

I ran back to my corner, my heart nearly beating out of my chest, hoping that people still thought I was a boy even though my long curly hair had fallen out of the cap. I got there, breathless and scared. How could I go back to being the main chef of the bakery when I didn't have my work clothes?

When I thought things couldn't get any worse, I saw Victor Veer. I crept closer and was relieved to see it wasn't him at all, just an elderly woman with red hair. Then, I thought I saw him again, but it was just a man with a red cap. I couldn't live like this, thinking Victor Veer might pop out from any corner. And If I couldn't work, how would I ever pay for food?

Suddenly, I had an idea. I would sneak out tonight to retrieve my dress, and then I would have only missed one day of work. They wouldn't fire me over one missed day. Would they?

Chapter Fifteen

Oliver

"**O**ne more story, please, Grandpa!" I exclaimed, sounding like a little kid.

I didn't care if I sounded like the littlest kid in the world. I'd thought I might not have another living relative, and it turned out that my grandpa was under my nose all this time. And now, unbelievably, we were curled up on his bed, telling stories.

"Fine," Grandpa said, rubbing his eyes. It was ten o'clock at night.

Grandpa started his story. "When I was once young

like you, Ollie, I had dreamed of being a sailor. I would beg and beg my dad to let me go out on one of the sailboats in the harbor, and he finally gave in when I was twenty years old. Then I went to sailing camp for the whole summer.

"Your grandma was one of my sailing mates. The minute I saw her, I immediately fell in love. After many years, we finally got married and we had your mother. Still, we continued to sail. Your mother was very smart, but she always had her own opinions. We sent her off to sailing camp for three summers in a row. She started sailing camp when she was about your age.

"She loved to sail. It was her life. But then she met your father, and she forgot all about her love of sailing. I had many arguments with her about giving up sailing for your father, but she just wouldn't listen. Then, one day she got so mad that she said she never wanted to see me again. So I left the house and I never saw her except for when she came to my shop. But, even then, she refused to talk to me and she forbid me from talking to her family."

Then Grandpa rubbed his eyes, but this time he wasn't tired. He was crying.

"Is that why you didn't know about me or my sister?"

I asked.

"Your sister? Who?" he asked me, with a confused look.

"Oh, I don't know if she is um... uh... still uh... alive. Her name is Shirley." I said.

A slow smile crossed his face and he winked at me.

"Well, I'll be. I think I might know her."

Chapter Sixteen

Shirley

I slipped on my dark pants, zipped up my dark coat, tucked my long black socks into my pants, slipped on my hideous shoes, then pulled my cap over my head, grabbed a nail for picking the lock, and grabbed a flashlight. Now I was ready for anything.

I ran over to the bakery, and effortlessly pulled open the door. *Why would the door be unlocked during this time of night?* It was twelve o'clock! I tiptoed in, careful not to make a sound, and I headed over to the counter, where I could see the dress.

Chapter Sixteen

Not wanting to waste any time, I ran over to the dress. I guess somebody must have spilled something because I slipped. I caught myself on the counter, but scraped my cheek in the process. In my state of shock, I dropped the flashlight and it fell to the floor with a loud clatter. Then I heard footsteps coming. I tried to run but I slipped and hit my rear end on the hard floor. It hurt so badly. I wanted to cry, but I hurried to my feet just as he approached. *He* was Roberto, the owner. I knew I had to face him.

"Shirley, why are you in those tattered boy clothes? Why is your cheek bleeding? Why are you in my bakery in the middle of the night?" he asked.

"Um, ur, uh," I was speechless.

"Shirley, come with me to my office," he said in a stern voice.

I followed him to his office and sat down on a wooden chair that creaked whenever I shifted. He sat down on the other chair, put his glasses on, and readjusted his tie.

"Shirley, why weren't you here today?" he asked.

"I was... sick." I lied.

"Well, you know the rules. You have to call in sick," he said.

"Um, I don't have a telephone in my, uh, where I live."
I said.

"Well, couldn't you have walked over to a booth?" he
questioned.

"I was too weak," I said, getting more nervous.

"Then why are you here now?" he asked.

"What's your point, Rob?" I asked

"Ms. Tark, for you, I am no longer Rob, I am Mr. Rouge,"
he said.

"What is this all about, Mr. Rouge?" I said.

He waved his hand at the door where a girl stood.

"Shirley, I would like you to meet Camilla Walter, our
new main chef of the bakery."

Camilla smiled a happy smile. She was a few inches
shorter than me and had perfect straight blond hair that
was tied neatly into a pink ribbon at the back of her hair.
Her skin was a bit lighter than mine, a lovely shade of snow
white. Her cheeks flushed pink when I turned to look at her.
Her lips were rosy red. She had no pimples, bruises or cuts
anywhere. Camilla Walter was *perfect*.

I was in such a trance that I didn't notice Rob talking.

"Shirley? Shirley?!" He finally got my attention.

"Yes," I said.

"Your work is no longer needed here."

I hung my head, mad that he had been so cruel. Still, I knew better than to argue.

As I was leaving, Camilla pulled me aside.

"Hey Shirley, I'm so sorry about this whole thing. Please don't be mad at me," she said, her voice sounding as sweet as honey.

"I'll be fine," I said glumly and started walking away.

"No, wait, Shirley," she said.

I stopped and turned back to her.

"My aunt, Colleen, has a very popular catering service. She needs a chef, and you can do all kinds of stuff there. I wish I could work there, but my aunt says I need to have my own life, so now I am working here. But I still get to help out on the weekends!" she said excitedly.

Did everybody in her family have a pretty name? I wondered.

"Thanks so much, Camilla!" I said.

I liked how her name rolled off my tongue.

"Oh, Shirley, you don't have to call me Camilla, call me Camille," she said.

I strolled out of the bakery feeling something that I had never felt before. I felt as if my heart was floating. Why was I feeling good if I had just been fired? I realized how good it felt to finally have a friend my age. That night, I thought about how excited I was to have Camille Walter as my friend. In a few years, we would probably be best friends and we would talk to each other all the time. I hadn't had a friend my age since I was eight years old!

Chapter Seventeen

Oliver

Grandpa and I were going to eat breakfast at Colleen's Diner, a place run by some old lady named Colleen Walter.

"Oliver, I have to tell you, you are going to love this place so much. It has fresh and healthy food and great service!" Grandpa exclaimed.

An old woman greeted us as we walked inside.

"Hello gentlemen, how do you do?"

She had straight blond hair with only a few streaks of grey, unlike Grandpa whose head was covered in thin grey hair. Her face showed no sign of wrinkles, and her skin was a pale snow white. She wore a pink dress covered with purple flowers, and purple flats. She must have been Colleen.

"We are doing well," Grandpa said.

"Oh, let me introduce you to my niece, Camille!" Colleen said.

Camille looked exactly like her aunt. She had perfect straight blond hair that was tied neatly into a pink ribbon at the back of her hair. Her skin was the same pale shade as her aunt, and she wore a matching pink dress with the same shoes.

"How many in your party?" she asked.

"Just two," I said.

"Okay! Right this way," she said and she led us to a table. The diner had fruit and vegetable wallpaper and you could even look out the window and see the real garden that they grew to make their food!

We sat down and I began flipping through the menu as fast as I could. I was hungry! I decided to order some waffles with blueberry sauce, and Grandpa chose eggs with grilled tomatoes. He asked me if I would order for him, because he was going to go to the bathroom. Then, another waiter came by and poured us some water.

"Have you decided on some food?" she asked politely.

She had chocolate brown eyes, and about the same color skin and hair as mine. I looked over at her nameplate. I couldn't really read what it said because it was so small, but it looked like "Tracy."

I ordered our food. Grandpa came back and the second we got our food, we devoured it. Then we got some hot cocoa and then we left. After going about one block, I realized I had forgotten my jacket, so we went back while Grandpa waited outside.

I ran over to the table and grabbed my jacket. I started to walk back, but then I heard someone at the telephone booth,

"Oh, that rat? Yup, the dog was terrible. I mean, he peed on my shoes, so finally I kicked the dumb guy out. I left him on the street corner. Yes, the one by the candy shop. Oh, no but I will get him back... Because I need him, you fool. How? I'm gonna go to the party. The dog just loves parties. I bet he'll walk right in. Oh yeah, that boy. Yup. I'm sure he has that dog. His relative is pretty rich. He'll be there. With the dog," he said.

As I listened, I realized the man on the phone was Victor Veer, the scary guy with the red bandana. I ran out of the diner as fast as I could.

"Grandpa?" I asked.

"Yes Olli-O," he said. That was his new favorite nickname for me.

"Um, are you going to a party anytime soon?" I asked.

"Yes. Tomorrow, actually. Why?" he asked.

"Oh, because um, I uh... nothing." I said.

I hoped that if this was the same party, my mutt would show up, but Victor Veer wouldn't.

Chapter Eighteen

Shirley

Because Camille and I were going to the party, we decided to wear our best clothes so that people would take us seriously. We weren't cooks this time because her aunt had invited us. We had both taken baths and were now in Camille's closet, trying on clothes. Her closet was perfect, painted pink with so many different outfits of different colors and styles.

"Did you hear that this is a very important adult party? We have to look our best!" Camille said, as she picked out a red dress with white heels.

She braided a red ribbon into her hair.

I picked out a puffy navy blue dress with polka dots, a white hat, and white heels with bows at the top. Camille frowned at my hair and took it out of the hat.

"Shirley, why do you hide your curls? They are beautiful!"

She braided a small section of my hair and placed around my head like a headband, then she brushed out my wavy curls, and I had to admit, I did look pretty with my hair down. I tucked my lucky family photo into my dress. Then we walked into the car. Her aunt said that she had forgotten something, so she went back into her house.

"Hey Shirley, I almost forgot! My aunt said that she could drop you off at your house. Where do you live?" Camille asked me.

"Um, Camille... do you have to promise not to tell anyone?" I asked.

"I promise, Shirley," She said.

"Well, I... um... don't have a home," I said.

She gave me an understanding smile. "Shirley, I know how hard it is when your parents get divorced and you have to live at two different houses. My cousin's parents are divorced." She said, "But which house do you prefer to be dropped off at?"

The longer this took, the harder it was to say. "No, Camille, my parents died seven years ago. I live on a street corner." I wiped a tear from my cheek.

Her eyes widened. "Really?"

"Yes."

"I didn't know," she said, her voice worried and sad. "I'm so sorry."

Her forehead creased, and I tried to figure out how to tell her that she didn't need to worry, that everything was okay.

But then she said, "Well, how about this? You can spend the night at my aunt's house for the next few months. I'll tell her your parents are away."

"Really?" I couldn't quite believe what she was offering. "Do you think that would work?"

"Sure!" said Camille.

I was speechless for a moment. Finally, I opened my mouth to say, "Thank you so much, Camille. You are a true friend!"

"You're welcome. You are the first real friend I've had in ages. My parents are always away, so I just stay with my aunt and I haven't had any time to make any real friends. You've been the best one so far. I hope we stay friends forever!" she said.

Colleen slipped back into the car. "Sorry, I just couldn't find the chocolate I was supposed to give to the host of the party. He was my old teacher in pastry school!"

Camille asked her aunt if I could stay with them, and her aunt said, "Oh sure, as long as it's okay with your parents, Shirley!"

Camille and I exchanged glances and both said at the same time, "It is!!"

I squeezed Camille's hand. Even after her aunt said yes it took me a minute or two to realize I actually had a temporary home now.

Chapter Nineteen

Oliver

Because this was a very fancy party, Grandpa and I had gone through his closet to find the fanciest thing he had from when he was a boy. Finally he found some black pants and a collared shirt, which was a bit too big for me, but it didn't matter because I was going to tuck it in.

"You know, I remember what it was like being a boy. I would always beg my dad to go to fancy parties with him. Whenever he said yes, I would always wear these collared shirts. I was fifteen at the time, and I loved to talk to the adults who would share their stories with me. Today, at the party, maybe you will do that!" he said.

I put on a fancy vest. Grandpa brushed and parted his hair, and then mine. He shined my shoes, and we were ready to go. We skipped into the car, and he drove us to the party.

When we got to the house, I gasped. It was bigger than anything I had seen since I lived in a house with my parents. Actually it was even bigger than my old house! It was four stories high and each floor had three balconies. From the car, I could see the velvety red curtains tied back revealing a sparkling chandelier made of jewels in nearly every room! Before we went inside, Grandpa lectured me about how I should be polite and courteous at the party, and how we were guests.

"Oliver, I know that you are a very responsible young man, fifteen years old as well. But you need to remember the rules of coming to a party. Rule number one: no running, jumping, or skipping. You may only walk. Rule number two: show your respect for the host by calling him "sir." Rule number three: don't eat too much. Rule number four: talk to your elders respectfully. Rule number five: enjoy yourself and have fun!" he said, playfully punching me in the arm.

Chapter Twenty

Shirley

"Good evening, sir," Camille and I said to the host of the party, who was sitting in a chair right in front of the entrance to the house.

He was a chubby man with a curly moustache and a friendly smile. Next to him, his wife sat in a chair with a cookie in her hand. She was also chubby and had loads of jewelry on, from diamonds, to emeralds, to rubies. From necklaces, to bracelets, to earrings. She was totally loaded. I wished I owned that much jewelry!

"Oh, you look so grown up, ladies," he said. "How old are you two?"

"Fifteen," we both said at the same time. Camille squeezed my hand and we both forced back laughter.

We walked into the house, which looked more like the White House than any ordinary house I'd ever seen. It was probably bigger, though! The walls were painted a fine gold, and the floors were lined with a velvety red carpet that Camille and I let our feet sink into. There were people everywhere, socializing, and some couples were slow dancing. Everything looked so grand. Camille and I were in awe. Our eyes were wide and our mouths gaped open.

Finally, after we stopped admiring the mansion, we grabbed some plates, and piled them high with cookies, cakes, sandwiches, and rolls. My stomach was very happy. This was the first time in a couple of weeks that I had had real food! Camille and I sat down at one of the tables and began to talk.

"So, Camille, do you attend school?" I asked.

"No, my parents don't really care about my education. They just want to marry me off so I am out of their hair. My aunt, Colleen, tries to teach me, but my older brother who's in college says I'm as dumb as a doorknob," she said sadly.

"You have a brother?" I asked,

She had never mentioned anything about him before.

"Well yes, but I feel like I'm not related to him because he steals all of my parents' attention and he treats me like his pet. Sometimes he's nice to me, but sometimes he's mean. What about you? Do you have any siblings, Shirley?" Camille questioned.

"Well, I had a twin brother named Oliver, but we haven't seen each other since our parents died when we were eight," I said, "I'm not sure if he is still alive though."

Then, out of the corner of my eye, I saw something brown running across the dining room. A wave of panic followed. It was my dog! What was he doing here? If he made a big mess, I would be in big trouble, and even worse, I couldn't imagine what they would do to him!

Chapter Twenty-One

Oliver

Grandpa and I got out of the car and greeted the host.

"How do you do, sir?" I asked.

Grandpa said I should have very good manners around elders, and I figured this man looked old enough to be an elder. He was chubby and talked like Grandpa, so he must have been. His wife sat next to him, wolfing down a mini cake. She was very chubby too. I wondered how this man had the patience to greet every guest who arrived. This seemed to be a very big party with a lot of people wearing very fancy clothing and talking like civilized adults.

"I'm doing very well. You sure look stunning, young man. How old are you?" he asked.

"Fifteen," I said.

"Ah, some fifteen year old girls just passed by, maybe you would be interested to talk to them," he said, with a slight smile on his face.

Once we got inside, I looked around. I didn't see the mutt, but out of the corner of my eye, I saw Victor Veer. He was wearing a nice suit, and for a change, he didn't have his red bandana with him. I stared in shock. I had heard him talking on the phone about being here, but I hadn't known if it would be this party, or whether he'd go through with his plan. I also worried about the mutt. What would happen if Victor found one of us alone? What would he do to us?

Chapter Twenty-Two

Shirley

I had to catch the mutt before somebody saw him.

"Excuse me, Camille," I said, "I've got to go to the bathroom."

"Is everything all right, Shirley?" she asked.

She probably read my panicked face.

"No, but you'll have to trust me about this, if I don't come back, don't worry about me. Just go to the candy shop." I said.

I thought that the candy shop would be the safest

place to hide if Victor Veer tried to do something to me, if he was even here. It would probably be safest if I was in a building close to my street corner where I had everything that was important to me. I had to protect my things while also keeping myself safe.

Following the direction I had seen the mutt go, I ran over to a side hallway. Suddenly, through the crowd, I saw a tiny patch of the mutt's shaggy brown coat. I dodged maids and butlers, and many other people. I must have not been looking where I was going, because the next thing I knew, I was on the floor. Not just on the floor, but on top of somebody's foot, with glass slivers in the side of my arm. I looked up. I had tripped a waiter, who had fallen over and spilled wine all over the hostess and the glass had fallen on me. I was in big trouble!

Right above me was Victor Veer. His golden tooth glimmered with delight.

Chapter Twenty-Three

Oliver

I had just put some bread rolls and butter on my plate, and I was just scooping up some chicken when I saw a brownish figure moving through the crowd. I tried to tell myself that it probably just someone else's brown coat. I knew it was the mutt and I couldn't deny that. I decided that no matter what I tried to tell myself, I wasn't going to take any chances in risking both my life and the mutt's life.

"Grandpa," I said.

"Ollie," he answered.

"If you don't find me at the party, just go back home," I said quickly, trying not to meet his gaze.

"Why? What is this, Oliver? I'm responsible for you! What if something happens to you? What will I ever do?" he said.

"Grandpa, just trust me this one time." I said impatiently.

I didn't want to wait for his response, so I just ran as fast as I could to the bathroom. I had seen the mutt run inside. I successfully dodged what seemed like millions of people talking and dancing. I looked over my shoulder to make sure that Victor wasn't following me, and went into the bathroom.

I slammed the door behind me.

Chapter Twenty-Four

Shirley

I was scared, but I had to catch the mutt before any more chaos found me, I wasn't willing to give up. I got up and chased the mutt into the bathroom and locked the door. I looked over at the wall. Someone was there already.

"I am so sorry," I said, my cheeks blushing.

I was so embarrassed; I had just walked in on a boy who looked about my age!

"No, I wasn't actually going to the bathroom. I just needed to get some fresh air," he said.

Just when I thought things couldn't get worse, my dog jumped up and licked him on the face.

"Don't mind my dog," I said, grabbing the mutt's collar.

The boy gave me a puzzled look. "What do you mean? This is my dog! He's been living with me for like two months."

"Same with me," I said, frowning.

"Oh," he said, his eyes confused.

Then I noticed something. I could see my mother's big brown eyes in his and his hair was curly like my father's and mine. It couldn't be possible. I was just dreaming. But the idea wouldn't let go of me.

"Sorry..." I took the photo out of my pocket and showed it to him. "Is that you?"

"What?" he stared at me for a moment before understanding flashed across his face. "Wait! I want to show you something."

He pulled out a necklace, "Do you know about this?"

"That's my mother's necklace!"

"Our mother's necklace," the boy said.

We exchanged glances, and then both said at the same time, "Shirley?" "Oliver?"

He threw his arms around me and we laughed and

cried at the same time.

Chapter Twenty-Five

Oliver

We hugged for a long time, until the dog started to bark. We shushed him, but he wouldn't stop. We heard footsteps coming. I hit the window with the toilet plunger and it shattered. Shirley, the dog, and I climbed carefully over the windowsill and ran the two blocks to the candy shop. By the time we got there, we were out of breath.

"Over here," I called to Shirley and the mutt, motioning to the cabinet nearby.

They rushed to join me and I grabbed a jar of toffees before we all squeezed inside and closed the doors. I told

Shirley about escaping from the orphanage and how I found the mutt. Then she told me about the diner and the bakery and how she had found the mutt. We told stories and ate toffees for a long time. Then we heard a voice.

"Ollie-O," the voice called.

If Grandpa was here, we must be safe. I exchanged a look with Shirley and opened the cabinet doors.

"Here, Gramps," I called as I got out of the shelf. "And I would like to introduce you to Shirley, my sister."

"Shirley, when Ollie told me he had a sister, I thought it must be you," he said. "I had no idea you were my granddaughter, all that time."

Our expressions said it all. Shirley had run into Grandpa's arms and was now crying happy tears. Grandpa was squeezing Shirley, the mutt, and me tightly, as if to never let go. I was sucking on a toffee and smiling the biggest smile ever. I thought my face was going to burst from happiness. And the mutt was wagging his tail and slobbering all over us, but we didn't care. We all hugged, even the mutt.

Then Grandpa made us some sandwiches and Shirley a peppermint sundae, me a banana toffee split, and him a hot fudge sundae to celebrate us all uniting.

Chapter Twenty-Six

Shirley

After a little while, we all settled down. Ollie and I looked through our family photo album and Grandpa started to listen to the radio. We were all sitting in the front room of grandpa's house which had brown walls, a fluffy white carpet, and looked like the meringue that Grandpa delicately piped onto lemon cakes, pies, and cookies. We were sitting on an old but soft brown leather couch, that smelled like Grandpa, in front of the radio.

The radio host was saying, "Give it up for the swinging

girlies! Now we will have our weather report. Good morning, Bronx."

The mutt wagged his tail and tilted his head up to the radio as if the reporter was speaking to him. A huge doggy smile spread across his face.

"Let's call him Bronx," Grandpa said.

"Yay, now we can stop calling him 'the mutt' and 'the puppy!'" I exclaimed.

"After all, he is a true New Yorker," said Oliver.

Bronx seemed happy with his name and so were we.

The next day, we played catch with Bronx in the field a couple blocks down from the candy shop. The field smelled like sweet milk and daisies. Surprisingly, Grandpa threw the farthest! We all shared stories and had a fun time. I invited Camille, Jerry, and Ruthie over, Grandpa invited Colleen, and Oliver got Bronx a collar and registered him to be our pet!

Chapter Twenty-Seven

Oliver

I woke up to the sound of screaming and yelling, and the sight of my sister banging on my door. Grandpa had given me my own room, up in the attic. It wasn't painted, and it had a low ceiling with cobwebs and smelled like mice. I shuddered. I leaned back on the surprisingly soft pillow that I slept on. I had to put my head on a certain spot of the pillow, otherwise the goose feathers would fall out of the hole that Shirley had failed to sew shut. I quickly ran out of bed, banging my sore head on the low ceiling like always.

"What is going on?" I asked Shirley.

"Shut up!" she whispered.

"Victor Veer is down there and he is trying to steal Bronx," she whispered with a worried look on her face.

"But he can't," I said, confused. "We already registered him as our dog!"

"It doesn't matter, Ollie. We have to stop him," she said, her eyes glinting with fear.

We crept down the stairs to where he was. He was trying to drag Bronx out. The mutt was frozen with fear and anger.

Shirley counted to three, and on three we leapt. I landed on Bronx. He was not very happy about that. But Shirley thankfully landed next to Victor. Though Shirley was a girl, she was about ten times stronger than any boy I had ever seen. She was even stronger than Russell Redlock, the bully at the orphanage. She jumped on Victor's back and pulled his underwear up so high that he screamed. Then Shirley bounced up to his head like a graceful flying monkey and pulled his long, thick, gnarly hair. Instead of screaming, Victor took his gun, and slammed it against Shirley's hand. Unfortunately, Shirley's hand was still ripping out his hair, and she didn't see the gun coming. On impact, both Victor and Shirley fell to the ground with a thud. Victor screamed. Shirley took one look at her hand and fainted. Her right hand had been shattered by Victor's gun.

We left the mutt with one of Grandpa's neighbors and rushed Shirley to the hospital. Everything in the emergency room was gloomy. Nobody was happy. It was deadly silent, except for when I heard the shrill cry of a newborn baby. There were all kinds of doctors hovering around the unconscious Shirley. Finally, the doctors finished examining her. A doctor with a nameplate that read *Dr. Green* explained to us that he was a surgeon, and that most of the bones in Shirley's right hand had been broken. He said he would have to do surgery to set the bones, and that it would take several months to heal. Before he left the room, he told us he would be back in about half an hour to take Shirley to the operating room.

It had been three hours since she had fallen unconscious. Why wasn't she waking up? I began to weep, and weep, and weep. I had already lost my mother and father. I couldn't bear the thought of losing my sister. I put my head on my grandpa's shoulder, drenching his neat collared shirt

Chapter Twenty-Eight

Shirley

I was dancing on the clouds like a happy fairy princess. I giggled. I love clouds. They're so fluffy and wuffy and puffy.

"Hehe," I giggled.

Then I saw them, the gates of heaven.

"Mmmmmooooommmmmyyyyy!" I shouted, "Ddddaaaaddddyyyyy!"

"Sssssshhhhhiiiiiirrrrrllllleeeeeyyy!" they answered, but their voices sounded so far away.

"Coooommmmmeeee bbbbeee wwwwwiiiiitttttthhhh uuuusssss," they said, looking more handsome and gorgeous than ever. They looked like angels.

I tried running towards them, but a magical force stopped me. Pink fairy dust was pulling me back.

"Hehe," I giggled again.

Then I fell through the clouds, falling and falling into a dark hole.

I woke up, confused. Why was I lying down in a hospital bed with tubes through my arm? I wasn't sick, was I? Then I saw Oliver and tried to wave, thinking that he would tell me what happened. The pain was immense. I couldn't even lift my right arm. What had they done to me?

Then I realized that my hand was bandaged and there were rusty red bloodstains staining the white gauze.

"Ollie, what happened to me?" I asked.

"Nothing," he said.

"Well, I'm not stupid, you know. My right arm is hurting like heck!" I shouted at him.

"Don't talk, Shirley. Rest." He replied.

A doctor came in and gave me some painkillers, and before I knew it, I was up in cloudland again.

Chapter Twenty-Nine

Oliver

We stayed in the hospital for five days. After today, Shirley would be released! I asked Grandpa if I could go get a soda. He said I could, but I had to be careful not to get lost. I walked to the soda machine and got a strawberry soda.

I was walking back to Shirley's room, when I stopped, dead in my tracks, frozen. On my left, there was a room with its door open. Inside the room was Victor Veer. He looked so weak. His whole head was bandaged. He was asleep, but

I couldn't even hear him breathe. He looked so much worse than Shirley. He had tubes going through both of his arms and his head was about the size of a giant watermelon. The thing that I noticed, though, was that I saw something different about him. He looked peaceful, just sleeping there, as though he could never hurt a fly. I almost forgave him. I just stood there, with my mouth wide open, until the nurses told me to go back to Shirley's room.

I decided not to tell Grandpa about Victor Veer, so I waited quietly until the nurses took all of the IVs out of Shirley, re-bandaged her hand up, gave her more painkillers, and helped her get dressed into her regular clothes. We drove back home.

"Ollieollieooops!" Shirley said.

"Yeah," I said.

I thought the medicine must be making her a bit wonky.

"Cccccccaaaaaannnnnn yyyyyooooouuuu dddddrrriiivvveeee mmeeeee uuppp ttoooo tttthhhheeee ccclllloooouuuddds ttooo sssee mmmoommy aaaannnddd ddddaaaddddy?" She questioned.

Yes indeed, the medicine was making her really

wonky. I decided not to respond to her, so we drove back home silently, except for Shirley, who kept gurgling like a baby.

Grandpa and I lifted Shirley into Grandpa's bed, so he could watch her and make sure that everything was all right. Shirley slept through two whole days! She kept asking us if she could go to the clouds to see our mom and dad.

Finally, after her two days of sleeping and eating mushed up bananas and peas, Shirley was better. That was when I decided to bring up the topic of Victor Veer. Shirley finally remembered who he was, how he crushed her right hand, and why she had gone to the hospital.

"Grandpa and Shirley," I said, trying to get their attention.

"Yes?" Grandpa asked.

"I'll be there in a minute, I'm just feeding Bronx," Shirley said.

Even though the doctors had told Shirley not to use her right arm for a couple more weeks, since they said she was a very strong little girl, Shirley seemed to be fully recovered aside from her hand. She was even planning to play a game of one-armed basketball with me over the weekend, and she was not planning on losing.

We all sat down on Grandpa's soft leather couch in front of the radio. The couch smelled like Grandpa.

"When I was going to get my strawberry soda, I know that you told me not to wander, Grandpa, but I saw Victor Veer!" I blurted out.

"What did he look like? Was he okay?" Shirley asked.

"Shirley, are you mad? He almost killed you! Why would you be worried about him?" I shouted, clearly confused.

"Well, Ollie," she said, her voice sounding like warm dripping honey, like my mother's voice, "I have always believed that everyone is human, and they all deserve a second chance. I'm not saying that what Victor did was right, but I am willing to forgive him," she said.

I was surprised!

"Oh, really? You talk about forgiving people, but you never forgive me, even if I accidentally trip you!" I exclaimed.

"Well, talking about Victor Veer..." said Grandpa, who clearly had something on his mind, butting in on our fight. "I have some things for you from the police, from when they found Victor Veer and took him to the hospital."

He put the objects on the ground. I thought they would be poison or something, but instead, they were two very familiar objects. A diary and the smashed metal dog bone from Bronx's collar. We opened the diary and began to read.

From the Diary of Victor Veer

Dear Diary, March 5th Thursday

That idiot, Joseph Tark, the owner, just fired me from Pinwheels and Threads. I could've become rich. I could've made a fortune, but no, Joseph just had to fire me. We were best friends until today. We knew where each other lived, all of our deep, dark secrets, and never fought. Until today, that is.

It started when he hired someone named Benny Talbot as the Executive Director of the company, instead of me. Back when we were both twenty years old, he had just graduated from college, and I was going into my third year of college. We both had the amazing idea of starting a company to produce fabric and threads for the top designer clothing companies. Since I was more focused on my college work, I told him he could start the company without me. He agreed, but said that once I graduated from college, he would immediately hire me as the Executive Director of the company. But I graduated from college two years later, and he had already found someone named Tate McNickles for the job. He promised me I could work for him if I wanted. Not wanting to ruin the friendship, I said I would work for him on one condition: he had to fire the Executive Director before ten years was up.

Well, today was the mark of ten years, and he fired Tate, but then hired Benny Talbot. I demanded he put me in the Executive Director's position and remove Benny, but he wouldn't listen. He said that Benny would work for him as the Executive Director for half of the money that I wanted to be paid. At that point, I demanded a raise of $1,000. Instead, he paid me $100,000 and told me I was still his best friend, but my work would no longer be needed there. I know I have to get revenge somehow...

Chapter Thirty

Shirley

"**S**o that explains why he was mad at Mother and Father!" I said.

"Oh," Ollie said, finally getting the whole diary entry.

I rolled my eyes at him. "Took you long enough."

"Whatever."

"Kids, I have something to confess to you," Grandpa said, his face suddenly serious.

"Yes?" I asked, worried.

"The reason why you probably don't remember me is

that your mother and I got into an argument. She was so mad at me for trying to force her to sail that she told me I was controlling her life and she didn't want to see me again. Even though I wanted to love you and talk to you like a true grandfather would, I respected her decision. Then, when I found out your parents had died, the policemen said I wasn't an authorized guardian. I searched for you anyway, but I couldn't find you. I'm so sorry. I left you alone for seven years. If I could've, I would've found you. I'm so sorry," Grandpa said, his eyes welling up with tears.

"It's okay, Grandpa," I blurted out. I thought it would make him feel better.

"And besides," said Ollie. "We're with you right now, and we'll never be separated again!"

It was true, now that I thought about it. I had a real family! I had Bronx, Oliver, and Grandpa!

There was still much more of the diary to read, so I flipped through a couple of pages until I found something that I thought would be interesting.

From the Diary of Victor Veer
Dear Diary, March 13th, Friday

I just crept into the Tarks' house. I was looking for their money. I tiptoed up the stairs and into the first room I saw. I heard two people talking; I recognized Joseph's annoying squeaky and fake voice instantly.

"Honey, you know we are being threatened by Victor. He could kill us any minute now. He's an evil, greedy fool, and he wants our treasures!" Joseph said.

Why would I be evil? (I had only murdered something when I was seventeen. I murdered my brother's pet parrot, which kept calling me stupid.) When did I threaten them? The last time I spoke to Joseph was last week when he fired me.

Sure, I threatened that I would get revenge, but I wasn't specific. Maybe they did have a point. How would I get all of their money without them calling the police?

"Joseph, dear, who will we pass our treasures on to? We surely cannot trust our own children, for they are only eight? I definitely do not trust my father, he will use all of the riches on his stupid candy shop," Barbara said.

Why did they keep using the word "treasure?" What kind of treasure, I wanted to know?

"Well, we can put our jade sphere with the pink

diamond spiral in our safe deposit box," Joseph said.

"But how will we hide the key? You do know that it is worth one million dollars!" Barbara questioned nervously. I knew that I had to steal both their money and the jade sphere with a pink diamond spiral. I needed it.

"Well, I have a crazy idea, but I know that it will work," Joseph said. "We can hide the key in Charlotte's dog tag," he said.

Then, he called their ugly mutt named "Charlotte" over to him. Charlotte came. He took the metal dog bone off of her collar, and placed a three dimensional dog bone on her collar. He took out the golden key to the safe deposit box, opened the dog bone dangling from Charlotte's collar, put the golden key into it, and snapped the dog tag back together with his bare hands.

"See, now it is sealed," he said.

I noticed that he snapped it back together at an angle, so now the dog tag could never be opened again. Now, I knew exactly what I had to do to get the money and the treasure. I had to murder them so there would be no proof of me stealing it.

I took out my black gun, aimed for their chests, shot,

and knocked them dead to the ground.

Chapter Thirty-One

Oliver

I picked up the smashed up bone from Bronx's collar. I could tell there was something inside it. I reached my pointer finger and my thumb into the crushed metal bone and pulled something out of it. It was a small golden key with the numbers 0130 engraved in such a tiny print that I had to squint to see them. This must have been the key that Victor was talking about in his diary, the key to our safe deposit box that held all of our parents' leftover money and valuable treasures. Then it all made sense.

"This is the key to the safe deposit box," I said, showing

Grandpa and Shirley who both turned their heads up from Victor Veer's diary that they were still reading.

"Victor saw the collar on Bronx, and thought that Bronx was Charlotte. That's why Victor kept stalking me when I had Bronx with me. When he attacked our house, he was so close to getting our treasures. It was all a perfect scheme. But something magical made the key end up in our hands, safely and away from Victor Veer."

"Do you think the treasures are still in the safe deposit box?" Shirley asked.

"I bet they are! I wish Mom and Dad were here to see this" I said.

"I think this calls for a triple fudge sundae!" Grandpa exclaimed. Bronx's

ea 3 perked up and his tail started to wag.

"No fudge for you, silly!" Shirley said laughing.

"But maybe a banana split!" I exclaimed.

Bronx bounded down the stairs. Grandpa took each of our hands and led us down to the shop.

About the Author

Sophia Nesamoney loves to play tennis, ski, dive, and travel. Her favorite subject at school is math, and in her free time, she loves to write, play the saxophone, and hang out with friends. While she was writing this book, her family helped her to never give up. Sophia is a seventh grader and she lives with her mom, dad, brother, and puppy in California. In the future, Sophia hopes to become a doctor and help people in need.